The Night of the Fireflies

by
Karen B. Winnick

Illustrated by
Yoriko Ito

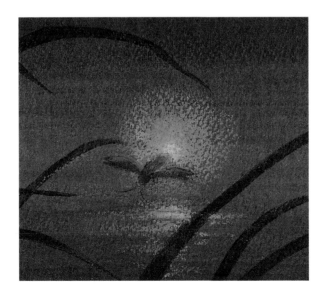

Boyds Mills Press

Published by Boyds Mills Press, Inc.
A Highlights Company
815 Church Street
Honesdale, Pennsylvania 18431
Printed in China

Library of Congress Cataloging-in-Publication Data

Winnick, Karen B.
  The night of the fireflies / by Karen B. Winnick ;
illustrated by Yoriko Ito. — 1st ed.
  p. : col. ill. ; cm.
ISBN 1563977257 (alk. paper)
1. Fireflies — Fiction. I. Ito, Yoriko, ill. II. Title.
  [E] 21   PZ7.W566Ni 2004
LC Control Number: 98088233

First edition, 2004
The text of this book is set in 13-point Stone Serif.
Visit our Web site at www.boydsmillspress.com

10 9 8 7 6 5 4 3 2 1

For my family and for Annie Sachiko Yasuda, a special little girl

—K. B. W.

For my favorite niece, Miyu-chan

—Y. I.

"What do fireflies look like?" Miko asked.

"You'll see." Her brother, Toshio, held up his lantern. "I've brought this to put the fireflies in. We can watch them glow for a little while."

Miko closed her eyes and tried to imagine the fireflies glowing in the lantern. Maybe she could bring them home, and they could shine in her room when she was alone at night.

Miko and Toshio walked, *clip-clop, clip-clop,* along the path through the woods.

"I hear voices," Toshio said. "Let's hurry." He ran to join the other children sitting in the clearing by the edge of the river.

"Wait for me." Miko reached out for his hand. "It's so dark."

Toshio hung his lantern on the branch of a tree and sat down. He joined in the songs of the other children.

Miko sat down next to Toshio. She clapped her hands and sang, too.

"When will we see the fireflies?"

"Soon," Toshio said.

A boy jumped up. "Look," he shouted. "The principal!"
The principal walked slowly into the clearing.
"What's in his box?" Miko whispered.
"Shhhh!" said Toshio.
Only the *croak-croak-croak* of the frogs rose from the river bed.
The principal opened the lid of his box a crack. A thin line of yellow light shone out.

"Tonight is the Night of the Fireflies," the principal proclaimed. He pulled off the lid.

Little lights flew out. They flew up and up and scattered in the sky. They began to blink and blink.

"Oh!" Miko cried. "Look how they sparkle!" She reached up to catch one.

"You need to chase them." Toshio ran off.

Miko hurried after a firefly. She chased it near the river's edge.

The firefly flew up over the river.

Miko watched its reflection shimmer in the water below. *The light seems to grow and grow*, she thought.

She chased another one back into the clearing. It flew out and disappeared between the branches of a tree.

"I caught another one!" shouted Toshio. He put it inside their lantern.

"I want to catch one," said Miko.

"Make a basket with your hands." Toshio pointed to a flickering light.

Miko put her hands together. She reached up toward a firefly.

"I caught it!" she shouted.

The firefly tickled her.

Miko laughed. She spread her fingers to peek inside.

The firefly's light blinked on and off. "It's my own little light," she said.

"Put your firefly in the lantern. I'll come get you when it's time to go." Toshio ran off again.

Miko carried her firefly carefully.

The light from the firefly lantern shone on her cotton kimono and her sandals. It lit up the branch of the tree and the tips of the pine needles. "Look how it glows!" Miko said.

Gently she lifted the top. She looked at her firefly, then put it inside. She stood back.

"I want to take you home, fireflies," Miko said. "I want to keep you." She took the lantern off the branch.

Miko walked toward the woods. Her arm shook as she stepped over crackling twigs and leaves that crunched. The trees stood around her like giants. Darkness was everywhere.

Miko shivered. "I need to find the path."

Whooooo, an owl screeched. Something scurried by and brushed the tip of her kimono. Miko jumped back. Her sandal stuck and she tripped. The lantern dropped. "Oh no!" she cried out.

The top came off and a few fireflies flew out. Quickly she put the cover back on.

"Miko!" Toshio hurried toward her. "I've been looking everywhere for you." He stared at the lantern. "Why did you take it?"

"I . . . I wanted to keep the fireflies." Miko began to cry.

Toshio picked up the lantern and gave it to her. "Here," he said. "You can carry it until we get home."

Miko and Toshio walked back through the woods. The glow from the firefly lantern lit their way as they crossed over the footbridge and followed the path to their home.

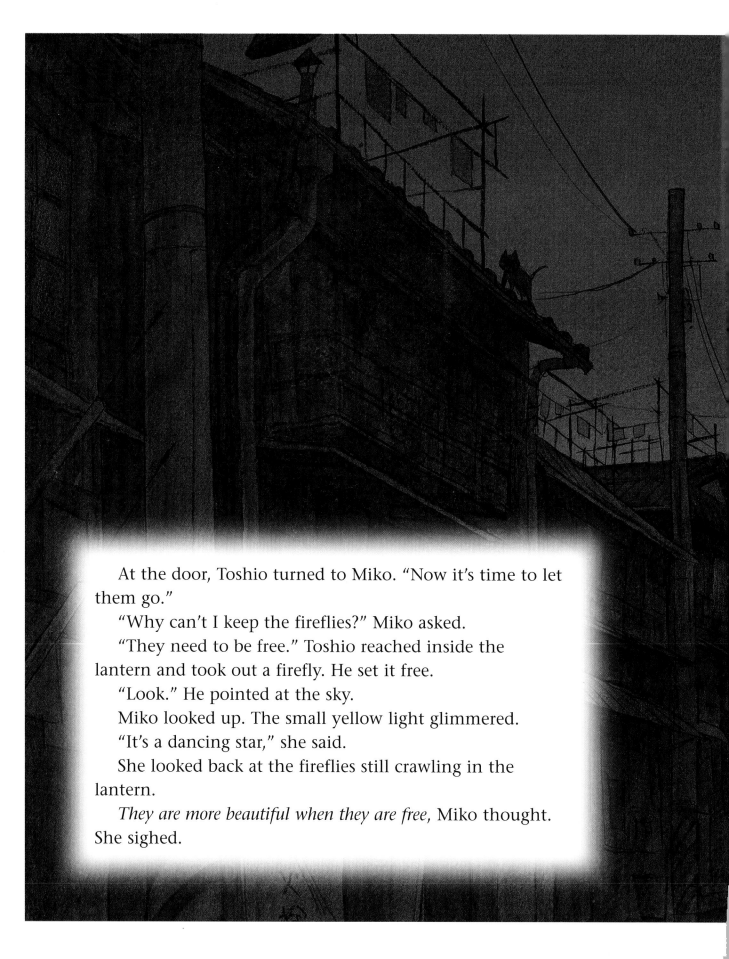

At the door, Toshio turned to Miko. "Now it's time to let them go."

"Why can't I keep the fireflies?" Miko asked.

"They need to be free." Toshio reached inside the lantern and took out a firefly. He set it free.

"Look." He pointed at the sky.

Miko looked up. The small yellow light glimmered.

"It's a dancing star," she said.

She looked back at the fireflies still crawling in the lantern.

They are more beautiful when they are free, Miko thought. She sighed.

She reached into the lantern and took one firefly out. She opened her hand. The firefly crawled to the tip of her finger. Miko watched it raise its wings and fly up. The firefly light began to dance in the sky.

"Good-bye," Miko whispered.
She took out another . . . and another . . .

A Note from the Author

Fireflies once filled the skies on summer evenings in Japan. But over time, many of the fireflies disappeared. Now they are raised and saved for one summer evening each year, when they are set free for the children.